Maggie's Missing Moonstone

A MAGIC LIBRARY COZY MYSTERY

MORGAN VALE

Maggie's Missing Moonstone

My name is Maggie Mason, and I'm kind of a klutz.

So when a talking owl shows up telling me I've been chosen to host this year's Lunar Festival, I don't really know what to think.

I'm a magical librarian, not an event planner. But it's a huge honor, and I'm not about to pass up this chance to improve my reputation.

Armed with my familiar cat Martin and my crazy family, we're going to make this the best Lunar Festival ever. There's just one problem...

The ceremonial moonstone? You know, the centerpiece of the whole affair? It's missing, and I'm starting to think someone stole it.

Yeah, I think I've got my work cut out for me this year. No pressure.

One

"**N**ow, where did I put that thing?"

My familiar Martin watched through judging eyes as I bent over double, digging through the pile of old boxes and paperwork in the cabinet. My name's Maggie Mason, and I'm a witch. Thing is, organization has never been my strong suit, and it's not exactly as easy as casting a clean-up spell.

So here I was, poring over piles of junk once again while looking for my checkbook. Don't ask me how I lost it — to be honest, I don't know how I lose half the things I do. They just seem to grow legs and walk off while I'm not looking.

I groaned and looked up from the mess to find Martin perched atop the counter, licking one paw and staring at me.

"I swear, you'd lose your head if it wasn't screwed on straight." He rolled over onto his back and started licking his tail. "And yet somehow you manage to remember all the moving pieces needed for magic. Figure that one out."

Okay, so maybe I had a bit of selective attention. Magic was fun and exciting. Keeping things tidy was decidedly...less so.

A knock at the door startled me and I jerked upright, knocking my head as I went. "Ahh—nuggets!" I cursed, holding the back of my head and wincing. The knock at the door came again. This was so not the time, but they wouldn't let up.

Still holding my head, I limped over to the door and opened it.

"Hello?" I called out. There was no one there. I looked down the driveway. Down the road. Nothing. Then what had—

"Down here," came the long-suffering voice.

It caught me by surprise. For a moment, I thought I was simply hearing things. But then I looked down at my feet, and saw an owl standing there, bedecked in a dapper-looking hat and bowtie. An overstuffed canvas bag slung across his body. When our eyes met, he flipped up a wing to his head in an approximation of a salute. "Air Mail here, special delivery for a Miss Maggie Mason."

"Air Mail..." I repeated to myself. I squinted at his wide amber eyes and no-nonsense demeanor. "Since when does Air Mail use owls?"

"In accordance with Ordinance 355.1, section 2b..."

My head spun. Bracing myself on the door frame, I held out my hand. "You know what, forget I asked. Just...give me the letter, or whatever it is. I need to lay down."

"Sign." He produced a clipboard out of seemingly nowhere and looked up at me expectantly.

"Are you seeing this, Martin, or did I hit my head a lot harder than I thought?"

Martin, my feline familiar, slunk down the hallway and joined me in the doorway. As soon as he saw the owl, he let out a high-pitched hiss. The owl reacted in turn, drawing himself upward and spreading his wings.

"Martin," I snapped, "This is not the time, and you know it. Now both of you, stand down."

When the owl relaxed a bit, I stepped out and signed the sliver of parchment dotted with all manner of bureaucratic nonsense. As soon as I was done, he dropped the letter, swiveled around on one leg, and flew off without another word.

I sighed and stepped back in, closing the door behind me.

"Back to the task at hand," I said to Martin, who glared at me, his whiskers twitching.

"You're not going to look at the letter?" Martin asked. He bumped his head against my leg. "After all it took to get to you?" He shook his head, wandering off. "Owls delivering the mail...what will they think of next..."

I looked down at the envelope in my hand. It could be anything. What if it was bad news? I'd had far too much of that lately.

I really had been working on pulling myself out of my funk, and just because I was reluctant to open an envelope didn't mean I was turning back to my old habits. I skimmed the envelope, noting that it was addressed to me and had that odd little seal on it: a crescent moon. After a moment of hesitation, I tore it open and removed a single piece of heavy ivory parchment.

"To Miss Maggie Mason--"

I read the letter aloud.

"We are pleased to inform you that you have been chosen as this year's host for the Lunar Festival. The Festival is a time to celebrate the cycle of the moon and the witching public's connection to the cycles of nature and the immortal Goddess. This year's festival will be held on a clear night this coming August 31st. We look forward to a most enjoyable festival, and hope to make your night a memorable one. Sincerely, the Cromwell Committee. P.S. Don't forget to bring your Moonstone. It will serve as the centerpiece for this year's Blessing."

I read the letter again. My heart skipped a beat. Hosting the Lunar Festival. All the witches in town would come. This was my chance to shine. To show everyone that I was more than a clumsy excuse for a witch.

I held the letter up to the light, squinting at it. The ornate writing seemed to swirl, as though the words were alive. Or maybe it was just my eyes playing tricks on me.

I felt a rush of excitement, though, and it wasn't lost on Martin. "Lunar Festival, huh?" He said. "That's a big deal." Martin strolled over and leaped onto the table, sniffing at the envelope. He wrinkled his nose. "Owls stink. Nasty creatures..."

"Oh, hush." I shooed him away. "Besides your feelings on that owl, what do you think?"

"Seems pretty clear to me." His sleek coat glowed against the sunlight, and he turned to me, his yellow eyes narrowed. His tail twitched back and forth. "If you're up for the challenge, it'll be a great way to start shaking things up around here. After all, you're more than the town klutz."

His words had stung, and there was truth to them. I didn't exactly have the best reputation around town. Goddess knew I tried my best, but I was always a little awkward. Little shy. Little weird. The other witches seemed to grasp things so easily, while I had to train and study for every little sliver of knowledge.

That hadn't stopped me, though. And the fact that the Committee would even let me host the Festival meant they were giving me a chance to prove myself. I couldn't let them down.

"All right," I said after letting out a breath. "Let's do this."

"That's the spirit," Martin urged me. "Now, what's the first thing we need to do?"

I glanced at the fridge. The beginnings of a headache echoed through my skull, and I knew if I didn't catch it now, I'd be in pain all day. "First, I'm going to get something to drink. My head is killing me."

Walking over to the fridge, I opened it and let the cool air wash over me. I leaned in to get the pitcher of water when I noticed something...

"Hey, how did my checkbook get in here?"

Two

I was surrounded on all sides.

No, not by would-be evildoers. By books.

During the day, I worked at the local library. Students from the school nearby came here to study, work, and learn more about the magical world. Books floated through the air of their own accord, and shelves were known to switch places when I had my back turned.

Made re-shelving the books each day really "fun."

The shelves lining the walls of the main hallway were filled with magical history. Ancient tablets, scrolls, and grimoires had been here for centuries, stacked next to one another. The smell of aging paper and the ideas within fueled my imagination.

It wasn't the most glamorous job, but it kept me busy and kept the lights on at home. Oh, and kept Martin fed, too. He wouldn't let me hear the end of it if I dared to get him the cheap food.

I had just kicked back at the circulation counter with a book on infusions when a figure appeared in my periphery. I looked up, scowling a bit as I had to put down my book. My face fell as soon as I saw who it was.

Rayna Willows. We'd gone to school together, and she never missed a chance to rub it in my face how she was doing so much better than I was. While I was working the day away in the dusty corners of the library, she'd earned a spot on the Alchemical Research Team. She was the shining star of the organization and didn't mind showing off every chance she got.

The door jingled, and she sashayed in, her long black hair swishing behind her. Her forest green eyes flashed, and her eyebrows rose as she swept her gaze across the room. When she settled on me, her ruby-red lips quirked up in a not-quite grin. More like a smirk.

"I heard the strangest rumor about you," she started. Rayna stepped closer and leaned across the desk. A glowing pendant dangled out from the neckline of her low-cut dress. "But it can't possibly be true."

"What did you hear?" I tried to sound as bored as possible. I kept my eyes on the book, but she didn't get the message. She was always doing this, and I didn't have it in me to play her games today.

"That you're going to host the Lunar Festival!" She stopped and tinkled out an annoyingly high-pitched laugh. "Isn't that crazy?"

My stomach clenched. I gave her the sweetest smile I could. "It's true."

Rayna stopped laughing. She stared. "What?"

"You heard me," I said coolly. "I got the invitation just yesterday. It's true."

She pursed her lips and stared at me like I was something she'd just scraped off the bottom of her shoe.

"That's...that's not possible," she said quietly. Her eyes narrowed.

"Sure it is. I'm a witch, just like you are. And you know as well as I do that they draw names from a hat every year. Just so happens it was me this time."

"But that's..." She sputtered, hands balling into fists at her side. "Why you?" She bit off the words like they were poison.

I was THIS close to rolling my eyes out of my head, but I managed to stop myself. "I don't know, Rayna." This was getting old. "But thanks for the vote of confidence. Now if you don't mind," I pointed to a flashing light on the desk, "Miss Caraway up on the third floor needs me."

"Hey, aren't you going to get my book on reserve first?"

I didn't know she had a book on reserve. "Let me go check the back shelf," I said wearily. "Be right back."

I pored over the small shelf in the back room where we kept interlibrary loans and holds. Each book had a card sticking out with the patron's name written on it for easy pickup. Try as I might, though, I didn't see a single book for Rayna. I looked under both her first and last name, but no dice.

With a sigh, I stood and returned to the desk empty-handed. I couldn't give her something that wasn't there, but she still wasn't going to be happy about it.

"Well?"

I winced. "I'm sorry, Rayna, but it looks like it hasn't been pulled yet. That, or it's still at another library."

"Seriously? I put in the hold over three days ago!"

I shrugged. "Sorry, it's not in the system. Can't give you something I don't have."

"Ugh!" she said at last. "Fine, I'll go look for it myself. This place is useless." Rayna turned on her heel and stalked off, her heels clacking across the tile floor as she went.

A long, feline yawn brought me back to attention as I watched her go. "What did I miss?" Came Martin's low voice.

I threw my hands up with a sigh. "You missed all the action!"

Martin simply tilted his head in question.

"Rayna came in," I added. He'd heard me rant about her enough times.

"Oh," he said flatly. "She give you any trouble?" Martin hopped up on to the desk and started sniffing my book.

I ran my hands through my hair. "Nothing I couldn't handle. Just her complaining about a book. Now come on, we gotta get up to the third floor."

"Fine, fine...." He muttered and followed behind me. "But if it's Miss Caraway again, you're gonna have to do the talking. She smells like fish...and not the good kind."

I snorted. What he didn't know couldn't hurt him.

On my way to the stairwell, I heard a crash and a subsequent squeal near the stacks. I groaned. Seriously...was she STILL here?

Martin followed me as I rounded the corner toward the rows of bookshelves. Sure enough, Rayna was standing there, hands on hips, with a pile of toppled books around her and a pissed-off look on her face.

"What happened?" I dared asking. I knew she was gonna give me an earful anyway.

Rayna glared at me. "What does it look like happened? I was looking for my book and then this cart collapsed on me!" She pointed at the overturned cart, which I could now see laying on the ground behind her.

"Uh huh." I wasn't buying it.

Rayna's face turned redder than her dress. "Can you...just clean this up!" She stomped toward me. "I could have been injured. Or worse!" Her voice rose an octave and I winced at the pitch. Martin hid behind my leg, but I could have sworn I heard a low growl.

"Is that..." She pointed one perfectly manicured nail at my ankle. "Is that your familiar? Is he threatening me?"

Okay. Breathe. I drew in a long, frustrating breath and let it out. "Just move out of the way, and I'll get everything cleaned up."

"Fine," she spat, "but I'm still not happy about this."

"Whatever," I mumbled under my breath. Rayna clacked away one more time, and this time I heard the door swish open and closed behind her.

"Why is she always so mean?" Martin asked. "You should have let me handle it. I would have given her a piece of my mind!"

"It wouldn't have done any good," I sighed, bending down to stack up the fallen books. "You know she lives in her own little world."

"Still, no one messes with my human like that." Martin sniffed at the books and looked up at me. "It's too bad I don't have opposable thumbs. Don't think the books would take well to a scratching, huh?"

"Aww, I know you just want to help." I bent down to scratch him behind the ears and finished stacking the last of the books back up on the cart. As I moved it out of the way back toward the shelves, I noticed something on the floor I hadn't seen earlier.

A small polished stone hung on a silver chain. I picked it up and looked it over for a minute. There was writing on one side, but it didn't look like any language I'd ever seen.

"This mean anything to you?" I held it out to Martin. He took a moment before he shook his head. "Looks like some kind of amulet. Pretty fancy. Wasn't Rayna wearing one of those?"

I squinted at it and looked at the writing again. "She had some kind of necklace on, but I didn't look too close..."

I held the stone out in front of me and twisted it in my hands, letting it dangle in front of my face. "I've never seen anything like this before. You think it has something to do with her work on the Alchemical Research Team?"

"If it does, you can bet she's going to be wanting it back sooner rather than later. Come on, let's see if we can catch her."

"Wait a second." I stopped. Looked at the amulet. Back to Martin. Back to the amulet. "What if she thinks we were trying to steal it or something? That seems like something she would try to pull."

Martin twirled his head upward in a circle — what I guessed was his rendition of rolling eyes. "Just put it in the lost and found box then, why do you even ask me if you're not going to listen?"

I sighed. "Yeah. You're right. Okay, I'm sorry Martin, I'm just being silly." I took the amulet off the chain and gently held it to my chest. "I just know Rayna...."

The cat huffed out an exasperated breath, took a few steps, and then scuttled off.

I swear, sometimes I think that cat's gonna be the end of me. Letting out an exhausted chuckle, I rushed after him. Don't let anyone tell you that working in a magical library is a sedentary job!

Three

I was so tired after work that day that I nearly forgot that I'd planned to eat dinner with my mom and grandma. I hadn't seen them in a bit and family dinners were always fun with the two of them bickering and bantering off one another, but I really didn't feel up to it tonight.

"Come on," Martin urged me. "If nothing else, it'll make for a good story. Who knows what Grandma Sam's gonna get up to this time?"

"Ain't that the truth." I shrugged on my coat and let Martin out the door before locking up and following him to the car. We were supposed to meet at my mom's house, but I thought about going over to pick up Grandma Sam first. She didn't have a car, you see, and insisted on getting around on a bright pink scooter.

Yeah, you heard that right. Can you imagine? I told you she was a bit odd, and that's not even the half of it.

So imagine my surprise when I got to mom's house and found her scooter already in the driveway.

Mom and Sam were playing cards, and they both looked up and smiled when I walked in. Sam was in her usual pink and yellow robes. My mom was a bit more subdued, wearing a deep mauve that highlighted her baby blue eyes. "Hey mom, Grandma," I said, giving them both quick hugs. "Where's dad?"

"He's probably out on the deck," Mom said, placing a few more cards in a pile on the table. Sam grinned broadly, her wrinkly old hands moving like lightning.

"Finally," she crowed. "I got you!"

Mom smirked and picked up the cards, shuffling them back into a pile. "And I'm not convinced you weren't cheating."

Grandma Sam chuckled. "Me, cheat? I am offended!"

Dad walked in through the back door, stripped of his usual business suit for khakis and a flannel shirt. His well-groomed hair was starting to show more salt than pepper, but you wouldn't tell it from his demeanor. My family was known for their energy, even late into old age.

"Hey honey!" he said, as he spotted me. His smile widened when he saw Martin, who I'd brought by his insistence. "Hey Martin, good to see you."

"Hey Mr. Mason," he replied. Dad and Martin had a good relationship -- probably because he liked to give Martin treats when he thought I wasn't looking.

I left them to it and turned to the card table, where another fast-paced round played out.

"Mind setting the table for us?" Mom asked. Sam shuffled the cards and they resumed playing. Grandma Sam puffed up like an angry bird as she lost a round. It was an equal mix of silly and adorable, but that's my grandma for you.

"So, what's on the menu tonight?" My dad joined me in the kitchen and I set out the plates while he poured drinks.

I tilted my nose into the air like Martin sometimes did. "Smells like spaghetti." It was a game we'd played since I was a kid. He would cook and then give me a chance to guess based on smell alone.

I'd gotten pretty good at it, if I do say so myself. But my father, ever the trickster, knew just how to push my buttons.

"Nope," he said with a grin. "Try again."

"What? Seriously?" I tapped my chin. "You sure you're not messing with me?"

His eyes twinkled. "Would I do that?"

"Am I supposed to answer honestly, or..."

My dad chuckled. "I'll give you one more guess."

I sniffed again. There was definitely something tomato-ey, but what? "Umm...lasagna?"

"Wrong again." His face lit up as he opened the oven. "Pizza!"

Hey, it was close enough. With the oven door open, the scents hit me full on. I hadn't realized how hungry I'd gotten, and my mouth watered. Even Martin noticed, peeking into the kitchen with wide eyes and a tentative meow.

"Pizza it is!" Dad declared, cheerfully sliding the

pizza off the pan and placing it on the table amidst plates and cutlery.

I rolled my eyes. "This game is as rigged as Grandma's card deck."

"I heard that!" Crowed Grandma Sam from the living room. We all broke into laughter as we sat down for dinner -- after all, that's what family was all about.

Despite everything, the pizza was delicious. Melty cheese and tomatoes and sausage on a slightly crispy thin crust. I was in heaven.

Ever since I was a kid, pizza was my comfort food. A good slice could wash away your worries, at least for a time. And when I was sitting there with my family, I almost didn't think about the looming festival or the run-in with Rayna earlier that day.

Almost.

Eventually, though, all good meals end, and we cleaned up the dishes from dinner. Everything was almost back in its proper place when Grandma Sam grabbed my arm.

"I heard about your invitation." It wasn't a question. Jeez, word really traveled fast around here. Grandma Sam's information network was almost as good as her scooter.

"Uh, yeah," I said. "It was...surprising."

"Not to me," she said, tapping her temple. "I knew you were destined for great things, my dear."

I couldn't help but snort. Great things, me? All I'd managed to do so far as a witch was be a great failure. I was happy enough, but it was hard when all my former classmates were powerful magi like Rayna.

"I can see you doubt me." She tapped her finger against her chin thoughtfully. "A pity, I used to be an excellent judge of character."

"You're still a good judge of character," Mom excused her gently, placing her hands on her shoulders and steering her off to the couch. "But it's getting late for the both of you. Come on."

After a round of goodbyes, Grandma Sam and I were back outside next to our respective vehicles. It was full dark now, and a chill settled over the neighborhood that my coat couldn't quite banish.

"It was good to see you again, Maggie." Grandma Sam brought me in for a hug, then crouched down to give Martin head pats. "You should come and visit sometime."

"Yeah, I know." I rubbed the back of my neck. "I've just been busy and all, and then with the Festival coming up, I'm--"

"Oh!" Her face lit up like she'd just remembered something. "I meant to ask you something, dear." Her eyes flicked to the door and then back to me. "Only, I wanted to wait until it was just us."

I gulped. What did she have up her sleeve this time? "Um...sure. What is it?"

"Your moonstone, dear," Grandma Sam said simply. "You'll need it for the ceremony."

I furrowed my brow. "I know."

"You know how I get those 'feelings' sometimes, right?" Her face slackened, turning serious. She shook her head. "Just...make sure everything's in order when you get home, all right?

"Okay..." I started. Anxiety already crawled up my stomach and into my throat. "Why, is something wrong? What did you see?"

"I'm sure it's nothing. Just my wild imagination again."

I eyed the infamous pink motor scooter and watched as she donned her helmet. That meant the conversation was over. "Are you sure you don't need a ride?" I asked, trying to stall for more time. "It's dark, and it feels like it could storm soon. You know I worry about you out there on the roads."

"I'll be fine, dear," she said, patting the bright yellow seat. "Besides, I'm taking the back roads."

"Cause it's safer?"

"Oh, heavens no." Grandma Sam laughed as she hopped on and the motor roared to life. "Less cops -- I can go faster and get away with it!"

I watched her go, like always, until the thrum of her engine faded. Then I climbed into my car along with Martin and sighed. "How did I end up with such a crazy family?" I looked over at Martin, who'd already curled up in a circle on the passenger seat.

"Who are you calling crazy?" He muttered, letting out a long jaw-breaking yawn. "Let's just go home. I'm tired."

I pulled the car out of the driveway and down the road, the headlights carving through the darkness. As the streetlights blurred past, my Grandma's words rang in my ears, mixed with Rayna's taunts and the formal wording of the festival invitation.

Was I really up to this? What if everyone was right, and I was just a screw-up? The Festival was one of the most important events of the year, and the ritual to gain the Moon's Blessing was essential for refining and accessing the magic in the surrounding air. Without it, we'd lose access to many of the things we took for granted.

The Moon's Blessing was the only way to tap the true gifts of magic that waited within all of us. The ability to practice magic safely and for the good of all.

No pressure.

I wanted to help people, but I'd only ever made a fool of myself. No more. From here on out, I was getting the job done. And that all started with the Moon's Blessing.

Four

"What was Grandma Sam going on about?" Martin asked as soon as we got home that night. "Something about a warning?"

I shrugged, trying not to reveal my nerves. "I don't know. Probably nothing. You know she has an overactive imagination."

"Yeah, but she sounded pretty serious to me. What was she wanting you to check on, anyway?"

"Oh, just my moonstone. Making sure it's charged in time for the festival and all that."

"...and is it?"

"Of course it is! It's right here in my bag." I held out my purse and unzipped it, reaching inside to find...

Nothing.

"Huh?" I muttered to myself, digging around a bit more. It should have been here. I carried it everywhere. I pulled out everything I'd had in there with it, and then looked inside. Nothing. I could feel the blood drain from my face.

"You were saying...?" Martin's voice roused me from my stupor.

"Oh, it's...it's not here..." I whispered.

"You're kidding me, right?"

I sat on the floor and spread out my things on the carpet. Martin moved quickly from hunting through my purse to checking all the pockets of my coat.

"It's not there, Martin," I panted, "I swear, it was in my bag just this morning!"

"Well, now it's not."

I growled and ran a hand through my hair. "Thanks, Captain Obvious. A little less snark and a little more help would be nice."

"What am I supposed to do? I'm just a cat, re-member?" He stuck his nose into small spaces like under the bed or the fridge while I looked...every-where else. My purse, my coat, my wallet, my makeup bag...you name it, I checked it.

My moonstone -- the source of my power and the cornerstone of the upcoming Festival -- was gone.

"I'm sorry..." was all I could say.

I covered my face with my hands. What was I going to do? The Festival was this weekend! It wasn't like I could just go and get another one. Moonstones were rare and powerful artifacts. Every witch had one, and it responded to that witch's power only. I still remembered when I'd graduated from the Academy and bonded with my moonstone in front of the whole school. It was a proud moment, a coming-of-age that all witches went through.

And now I'd lost it like an idiot.

Maybe Rayna was right. Maybe I was useless.

I slumped against the wall, staring at the ceiling and trying to still the tears that flecked the corners of my eyes. How could I have let this happen? A witch's moonstone was everything to her. The longer a witch went without it, the more their power could wane.

I had to find my moonstone, and fast.

"You're not going anywhere until you get some sleep." Martin chided me, just as the old grandfather clock in the living room struck twelve. "It's midnight."

I scrubbed a hand across my face again. He was right, I knew that, but another part of me said I had no time to lose. My mind was far too panicked to get any sleep right now. I had to do something!

"How am I supposed to get some shut-eye with my moonstone on the loose out there?" I raised an eyebrow.

"Calm down, first of all." Martin may be a smart mouth at the best of times, but he always had my health and happiness in mind. He gave me the truth when I needed it. Even when it hurt sometimes. "You'll be no good to anyone if you collapse from exhaustion." With a few steps toward the bedroom, he looked back at me and meowed. "Go get some sleep and we'll figure this out tomorrow, okay?"

I sighed, annoyed. "Fine. But I'm getting up early. We'll retrace our steps first thing." With a final yawn, I burrowed into the pillows and blankets. I wanted to stay awake, almost out of spite, but the moment I curled into the fluffy softness my brain drifted off, and I was soon fast asleep.

"Martin!" I shrieked when I caught sight of the alarm clock. "Why didn't you wake me up?"

"I tried to," he said, deadpan. "Seven times."

"What?!" Throwing back the covers, I bolted out of bed and to the closet to get dressed.

"Not my fault you were dead to the world," Martin explained. "I tried patting you, shaking you, meowing really loud next to your ear..."

"You--oh, never mind!" I schooled my hair into a presentable ponytail and pulled on my coat. "Let's go!"

Not exactly the best start to the morning, but hey -- it could only get better from here, right? After brushing my teeth and making sure I'd put everything back into my purse, Martin and I were out the door an hour later than planned.

As I revved the car to life and Martin settled in the passenger seat next to me, I ran through the events of the previous day. I'd woken up, eaten breakfast, driven to the library, parked, worked until lunch, went to the nearby diner, back to work, ran into Rayna, went home, and then to dinner with family that night.

It wasn't my busiest day, but the number of places I had to check still astounded me. One event stuck out like a sore thumb, though, and reminded me of another strange happening. My run in with Rayna wasn't exactly unusual, but the pendant I'd found when she rushed off was.

"Martin, check my bag. Is Rayna's necklace still in there?"

He dove in until only his ears were poking out. The chain dangled over one ear and the pendant covered his snout. "Yeah?"

"Good," I said without taking my eyes off the road. "I have an idea."

The sun was just starting to rise as the pair of us drove through the city streets. It was a beautiful autumn morning, crisp and clear and full of promise. Leaves still clung to trees in every direction, but they had started to turn color already. The air was cool enough to make the sunlight feel warm, and it smelled like fall.

"So, what's this brilliant plan of yours?" Martin asked after a while.

I glanced at him from the corner of my eye. "We have something Rayna wants. And she has something I need."

Martin was silent a moment, the only sounds our tires clicking over the drawbridge crossing the river. "So an exchange," he said at last. "You figured out how to use it to your advantage."

I nodded before taking a left at the intersection. Normally, I would turn right to head to the library for work, but today I had a different plan. "Let's just hope I'm right."

The ivory towers of the Alchemical Research Lab shot toward the sky on the other side of the bridge. The absurd amount of pearly white stone combined with the endless windows reflecting the early sun made it seem more like a palace than a laboratory. But then again, I figured, that suited Rayna just fine. She cared more about appearances and prestige than anything else.

I pulled to a stop in front of the main entrance and got out of the car. Martin hopped down beside me. "You can't be serious about this," he protested. "What makes you think you'll be able to see her, much less talk to her while she's at work?"

I reached into my coat and pulled out the pendant. The chain sparkled in the sunlight and the stone threw flecks of color on the concrete. "Because I have this."

Five

I'd always heard stories about the prestigious halls of the Alchemical Research Lab, but this was my first time actually visiting. It was even more grand than I'd expected. The Academy on the other side of the bridge was nice and all, but this place took things to a new level.

Even walking through the doors and down the long corridor to the lobby made me feel small and inadequate. Martin kept close to my side to avoid accidentally touching or knocking anything over.

The corridor opened up into a huge circular room with tall pillars and tapestries of every color in the rainbow. A large mahogany desk sat square in the middle, right under a magical chandelier that glowed with green flame. The walls, where tapestries didn't cover them, were lined with bookshelves. A rich, plush red carpeting rolled out toward the center desk and in the four cardinal directions. The real showstopper, though, was the massive glass skylight several stories above us. It let in the brightening sun, casting the entire building in a soft, golden light.

A man stood behind the receptionist's desk. Tufts of white hair puffed out behind his ears, but not much else. When Martin and I drew closer, he looked up and nearly jumped out of his seat in surprise.

"Oh, goodness!" He yelped, adjusting his glasses. I noticed only now that the man was an incredibly short fellow, sitting on top of several thick leather-bound volumes to reach the desk at all. "I'm so sorry! I didn't see you come in!"

Martin and I exchanged glances. This guy was clearly a bit off.

"My name is Roz," he continued. "How can I help you?"

"We're looking for Rayna Willows." Might as well get straight to the point. "Is she in today?"

He pulled out a strange-looking ledger and flipped through it, one long finger running down each page. "Ah! There we are." Roz snapped the book shut and looked back up at us. His eyes were like a bug's -- unnaturally magnified by his specs. "Yes, she is here today. No, she isn't taking visitors."

My face fell, but I'd been prepared for this. "Why not?" I asked.

"Well, she's working on a very sensitive project. Can't have any unauthorized personnel up there right now." Roz swiveled in his tiny chair until his back was to us, then started picking through a file cabinet. Apparently, that was the end of the discussion in his mind.

"We don't need to access the workshop," I pressed. When he didn't answer, I tapped on the counter with my knuckles. "Hello? We're still here."

Roz spun around again and sighed heavily. "Oh. You again. I've already said my piece. Good day." With a wave, he turned away from me and went back to whatever it was he'd been doing before.

I winced. I had one more thing to try, and if this didn't work...

"Rayna lost something at my workplace yesterday." I pulled out the amulet and dangled it in front of him. "I called to tell her I'd found and it, and she asked me to bring it to her here. Can you please go get her?"

Roz's eyes narrowed. The small pupils tracked the swaying of the amulet back and forth. "If you want to leave it here with me, I'll make sure that she gets it."

I shook my head. "No, I can't do that. She specifically asked me to deliver it to her personally."

The man frowned. "I'm afraid I must insist..."

I held up my hand. "Please," I interrupted. "It's important."

It didn't matter. He continued shaking his head, then pointed to the door. "I can't help you. You'll have to meet with Miss Willows outside business hours. Good day."

With that, Roz returned to the depths of his desk and the stacks of books surrounding him. I stared after him, but there was nothing else I could say. Defeated, I turned and headed back toward the doors. Martin and I walked side-by-side down the corridor, neither saying a word.

"What now?" he finally asked when we were halfway to the lobby. "You going to give up?"

I didn't even bother trying to hide the frustration in my voice. "Not yet."

"So what's the plan?" Martin's claws clicked on the freshly polished tile. Part of me, a cynical part, hoped he scratched up their nice floors.

"Well," I said, checking my watch, "we got a late start and wasted too much time here, so we won't be able to go to the diner this morning like I'd hoped. I'll call Peggy when I get to work and ask if she's seen anything. Maybe someone turned it in."

"Did you have it at the library yesterday?" Martin asked when we piled into the car. "Just trying to think of when the last time you had it was."

I tapped my fingers against the steering wheel, trying to think. "It's all such a blur...I think I remember seeing it in my bag at lunch, but...I don't know!"

At that, an alarm beeped on my phone. I growled and turned it off, putting the car into drive. "And now I'm going to be late for work!"

Six

When I arrived at the Arcane Library and got to my desk, my first visitor was someone I didn't expect: my grandmother.

"I hope you're not upset about the other night," she said, with a smile so sweet and genuine, it made me feel guilty. "You know I can go a bit overboard sometimes and worry about nothing. I wanted to come and check on you. Make sure everything was all right."

"Oh, Grandma! It's fine. Really." I smiled back automatically and tried to ignore the nagging feeling in my gut. She'd tried to warn me. Without even realizing it, had she known something would happen to my moonstone before even I did? I fought with the decision in my mind. Should I tell her what happened? Could she help?

"I'm glad to hear that," she said, patting my arm and giving my shoulder a squeeze. "Now, I need to grab a book. I'll see you later."

She turned toward the shelves, but I called out at the last minute. "Wait! There's...I wanted to talk to you about something."

When Grandma Sam made eye contact with me this time, she wore a knowing smile. "Oh?"

I took a deep breath and let it out slowly. "I think..." I started, not sure how to say it. "I think you were right."

She raised an eyebrow. "I often am...but what about?"

I looked down at Martin, who was napping on top of an encyclopedia. So much for backup. With a gulp, I added, "about my moonstone. I think...something happened to it."

Grandma's face went blank and her eyes narrowed. "What do you mean by that?"

"I...um. I can't find it." My face grew hot and I stared down at the desk, not able to meet her gaze. I knew I was a klutz. Everyone knew that. But losing something of this magnitude? That was bad, even for me.

"I've been looking everywhere," I continued, voice cracking. "In the apartment, my bag, the car..."

Her expression softened and she reached over and patted my hand. "Maggie...look at me." Her voice was soft. Not angry. Not condescending. I blinked away the tears gathering in my eyes and looked up at her.

"I'm sorry." The words spilled out like a waterfall now. "You were right. Something did happen to it, and I wasn't paying attention. I should have noticed."

"It's okay." She leaned forward and took my hand in her own. "Don't beat yourself up about it. You're just human. We all make mistakes."

I nodded, but my heart felt heavy. "But the Festival is this weekend!" I blurted. "And we still don't know if I can get it back or not."

My grandmother frowned. "We'll figure this out. Don't worry about it any more today. Just take care of your work and focus on what you want to accomplish. And we will find that stone, you'll see."

"Okay," I said, trying to keep my voice steady. "Thanks."

"You're welcome." She squeezed my hand again and stood up. "I better go. I've got a few errands to run, and Mr. Hendricks is waiting for me over at the apothecary." She glanced at her phone, and then nodded. "Why don't you meet me for lunch? Will you be able to get away for a bit?"

"Yeah. I have an hour for lunch and Violet can cover for me."

She smiled. "Perfect. I'll see you later, Maggie. Love you!"

"Love you too," I said as she headed for the door. "And thanks."

I watched her leave and sighed heavily. Martin stirred and opened one sleepy eye, then closed it again. He seemed content to stay that way for a while longer.

When she was gone, I sat there staring at the table, my hands trembling. What would happen if I couldn't find it in time? Would I lose my job? Or worse yet, my magic?

So much for proving my worth as a witch.

I swallowed hard and rubbed my eyes. I had to get back into the swing of things. It wouldn't be easy, but I could do this. I still had my family. I still had Martin. And I had a plan.

I grabbed my purse and set to work, pulling out my phone and calling Peggy.

"Hello?"

"Hi, Peggy! This is Maggie."

"Oh, hi! I'm glad you called! How are you doing?"

I smiled. "Good. Listen, I was wondering if anyone turned in a moonstone to the lost and found over there."

"A moonstone?" Peggy said after a pause. "You mean like, a witch's moonstone?"

I grimaced. "Yeah. Have you seen one?"

"Can't say I have." The sounds of the diner echoed on the line behind her. A man barked out her name. "Sorry, I've gotta go. I'll let you know if anything turns up."

"Thanks--" but before I could even finish the word, she hung up.

Wow. Today was not giving me a break!

I slumped down in my chair and stared at Martin's sleeping form. I'd never been so stressed out and exhausted, not even when I was studying at the Academy. Yet somehow, a spark of hope still flared within me. I was a witch, darn it! I didn't go through all those years of schooling for nothing. Magic flowed in the air and ran in my blood. I could find that missing stone. I could perform the ritual at the Festival this weekend.

I could redeem myself.

Because I had no other choice.

Seven

Lunchtime rolled around quickly enough. I told Violet I was taking my lunch and then stepped out into the courtyard with Martin. Grandma Sam was already there, waiting for me.

She waved and grinned, her eyes flashing with some hidden mischief. Her own moonstone hung around her neck on a beaded chain. Another pang of guilt rolled through me. Was I the only witch to ever lose her moonstone? Surely not, right?

Grandma motioned toward the bench next to hers and I sat down. Martin hopped up next to me. "You look tired," she noticed. It wasn't a question.

I let out a nervous laugh. "That's one way to put it. Shall we get lunch?"

"Way ahead of you." Grandma Sam opened up her purse and pulled out two matching bags. They were full of homemade sandwiches, freshly cut vegetables, and more. My mouth dropped open as she pulled more and more food out of that bag of hers. How did she fit everything in there?

The answer, as it was with most everything in this world, was simple: magic.

"I know you've been through a lot lately," she added. "So I wanted to bring you some lunch."

I didn't know what to say. "I...thank you." She was too good to me at times, I swear.

"I even brought something for Martin, too."

He perked up at that. She put a bowl of fresh tuna salad on the ground next to her and Martin dove in without hesitation. I watched him happily chow down, then looked back to my grandmother.

"You said you were going to help me look for my moonstone," I said between bites of my sandwich. Even though the food was delicious, a different hunger lodged in my gut and wouldn't leave.

She nodded and gave me a warm smile. "I am."

I blinked. Waited. Took another bite of my sandwich. Now was not the time to speak in riddles. I needed to know how she could possibly help me find it.

"How?" I asked, swallowing my words.

Her expression grew serious. "Maggie, listen to me very carefully. You are a powerful witch. What you lack is confidence."

Oof. That hit me like a physical blow. I winced, but she wasn't wrong. "I appreciate that, grandma, but how is that supposed to help me find my moonstone? A 'powerful witch' wouldn't lose such a thing." My face fell as I remembered Rayna's taunts.

"I'm not talking about your power," Grandma said gently, putting a hand on my arm. "What you need to focus on are your strengths."

"My strengths?" I echoed. The thought made me feel sick. How could I have so much potential, and yet still be so weak? "Like being a klutz? Or losing things on purpose?"

"No, you're not a klutz. Your problem is that you don't know who you really are."

I stared down at my hands. I'd been so focused on my weaknesses, I never stopped to think about my strengths. About what I stood for. What I wanted out of this life. And now, I was letting it all slip away from me because of a stupid mistake!

"Who do you want to become?" Grandma Sam's voice snapped me out of my reverie. I looked up and saw her staring at me intently. I couldn't stop the tears that welled in my eyes at the question.

I took a deep breath. "A witch. A good one. Not...an embarrassment."

"You already are a good one," Grandma Sam insisted. "Look at what you've done for me. For Martin. Look at everything you've accomplished. You are a good person, Maggie. With a little more confidence and some guidance, you could go far."

She smiled. I wanted to believe her. I wanted to trust her. But right then, I was just a mess of feelings that I didn't know how to sort out.

Martin nuzzled against me from one side while my Grandma soothed me from the other. "You want to know a secret?" She said quietly.

I looked up.

"When I was your age, I actually broke my moonstone."

My eyes widened. "You...? But you're the most powerful witch I know!"

She nodded. "And I made mistakes too, child. Got over ambitious, tried a spell too high level for me, and shattered the whole thing. It was a mess." Her smile faded, her eyes far away. "Thought my career was over. I'd never heard of anyone breaking a moonstone before. Like you, I was scared. I was embarrassed, and I didn't know what to do?"

"What happened?" I breathed. My eyes flickered down to the moonstone around her neck. "Did you fix it, or...?"

She reached up with both hands, running them along the smooth surface of the stone. "I was lucky. I was able to get it repaired. That wasn't even the hardest part, though. It took a lot of time and money to fix it up, but you know what took even longer?"

I shook my head.

"My mindset." She tapped her forehead. "How I thought about myself. Even after I got my stone fixed, I was scared to use magic for a long time. I wanted to avoid letting anyone down again. Least of all myself." She paused for a moment, then took my hand. "Do you see where I'm coming from?"

I swallowed the lump in my throat, wiped my eyes, and nodded. "Yeah. I guess I do." I turned back to Martin, who had finished his lunch and was busy licking a smear of mayonnaise off his whiskers.

"But you can't give up," Grandma Sam continued, giving me a firm squeeze. "Not now. You have so much to offer. So many people to help. Don't throw it all away because you're scared."

"Okay...okay. I'll try."

"Good girl," she said, smiling at me. "Now take my hands. Both of them. I want to try something."

I hesitated, but did as she asked. "What are we doing?"

Her eyes sparkled once more, and a grin stretched across her face. "Magic."

We sat there for a few moments, holding each other's hands. Then, slowly, I felt a familiar tingle in my fingers. It started there and spread further, up my arms. To my shoulders and neck. Down my spine. I shivered, feeling goosebumps rise on my skin.

"It's working," I whispered.

Grandma Sam grinned. "Yes! I knew it would." She squeezed tighter. "I want you to think about your moonstone, Maggie. Think about the last time you saw it. Try to think where it would've been. What it would've seen."

I furrowed my brow. "What do you mean? The moonstone doesn't have eyes. It can't see, or..."

"Can't it?" She challenged. "Humor me."

I frowned and closed my eyes. I pictured my moonstone. That warm glow that always surrounded me when I held it.

Dark, blurry shapes started to float through my mind. It was hazy at first, like a dream or trying to make something out underwater. But the more I concentrated on it, the clearer they became.

The tall stacks and floating lights of the library surrounded me. There was the circulation desk, and there was Martin, and...

The images shifted, and then I saw myself. That nearly knocked me out of the trance, to see myself like that. But my grandma's soothing words and touched kept me anchored to the moment. I let out a shaky breath and continued to watch the events unfold in my mind, like a old camera reel.

I was there. I was reading a book, and Martin was sitting next to me, asleep as always. Sounds filtered into the dreamscape. The sound of high heels on tiled floor...

The perspective shifted again, this time showing my purse. I'd set it on top of the desk and was looking for my reading glasses when someone cleared their throat, and I looked up...

I gasped. Rayna stood there, just as I remembered her. She pointed to the back room. I remembered her request well. I got out of my chair, went to check on her book, and then...

That's when everything changed. I recalled going to the back room to look for Rayna's hold, but the images didn't shift. Instead, they stayed focused on the counter. In particular, focused on the purse...

That's when I realized. I was seeing the scene from yesterday replay in my mind, from the moonstone's perspective! I struggled to hold on to the images. They faded further the more "I" drifted away, but before everything went black, I saw Rayna take a step forward, her long manicured fingers diving into my purse...

I came to with a gasp, yanking my hands away and breaking the connection. A fine sheen of sweat covered my forehead and I panted, wide-eyed, at my grandmother and Martin. My heart pounded in my ears.

"What did you see?" Grandma Sam asked quietly. I had a feeling she already knew.

The pieces clicked together like parts of a long forgotten puzzle. "I know what happened!" I exclaimed, jumping to my feet. "But what did you...?"

Grandma Sam regarded me warmly. "That was all you, dear. I simply gave you the belief you needed to cast the magic for yourself."

I stood there, speechless. I'd actually used my magic, and for once, didn't screw anything up! That, AND I knew where to find my moonstone! I glanced down at Martin, who let out an excited trill.

"Now do you believe me?" Grandma Sam said sweetly.

Warmth spread through my chest and a lump formed in my throat. It wasn't a sad or helpless feeling, though. It was the rare, buoyant power of hope. I smiled up at her, and she beamed back.

"Yes," I breathed.

"Good. Now, let's go get your stone. Meet me at the scooter."

"We already tried the ARL this morning. The snobby receptionist wouldn't let us in."

"Not with me, you haven't." Grandma Sam winked. "Let Violet know you'll be a bit longer. We've got a case to solve."

Well, I can say riding passenger on my grandma's scooter is officially on my 'never again' list. I tried to talk her out of it, but she wasn't having it. When she makes her mind up about something, no one can change it. Not even me -- and believe me, I tried.

Let's just say the ride did nothing to allay my fears of her tearing up the roadways by herself on this little thing. I thought these scooters weren't even able to go that fast!

Yeah. Never. Again.

The moment we pulled up to the Alchemical Research Lab and I got off the scooter, I'd never been so grateful for solid ground.

"Now wasn't that better than trying to find parking?" Grandma Sam asked me. Her hair was windswept and wild, but her energy hadn't waned.

"Uh..." I knew better than to argue. "Yeah. Thanks for the ride."

"More like no thanks..." Martin muttered under his breath. He wobbled drunkenly on all fours after the crazy ride. It was probably even more terrifying for him than it was for me.

"How'd you like the scooter, Maggie? Was it fun?"

"Loads," I lied. Time to change the subject. "Now what's your secret plan to get us in there so we can confront Rayna?"

"Oh, it just so happens I know a guy..." Grandma Sam didn't meet my eye. Was that a blush creeping up her cheeks?

"Grandma!" I yelped. "Are you...seeing someone?"

She looked away, but not before I caught the faintest hint of a smile on her lips. "Seeing is a bit of a strong word. But he does owe me a favor. Come on." She grabbed my hand and led me inside, her voice dropping to a murmur. "He works here, in security, no less."

That only formed more questions than answers, but I followed her lead. The lobby of the ARL was bustling with activity, and as usual, people were coming in and out. A few glanced our way, but most ignored us completely.

The splendor of the building was no less impressive the second time around. Instead of going straight to the center desk that Martin and I had approached, we hung a left down a side corridor until we appeared at a set of elevators. She tapped a panel on the wall and scrolled down a list of people until she found the one she was looking for. With another tap, a voice came on the line.

"Security here, what's the trouble?"

"Barney, is that you?" Grandma Sam said in an overly sweetened voice. "It's Sam."

A pause. "Sam? What are you doing here?"

"I need help with something. Can you come down to the lobby for me?" Even though there wasn't a video feed, she still fluttered her eyelashes. I covered my mouth with my hand and looked down at Martin, who mimicked a dry retch.

"Sorry Sammy, can't leave my post right now. But let me buzz you up. One of the guys'll get you sorted."

A mechanical buzz echoed from the panel, and with a ding, the elevator next to us opened.

"Thanks," she purred. "Be right there." And with that, the call ended.

She looked to me and Martin, still gaping at her. "Well, don't just stand there, let's get going!" We shuffled ourselves into the elevator, and with another ding, the doors closed around us.

"I've still got it," Grandma Sam said in a self-satisfied tone. "Now do what you need to do and let's get out of here."

"Uh, okay..." I had a LOT of questions, but now wasn't the time for answers. I tapped the panel like Grandma Sam had and navigated to the directory. It listed everyone who worked in the building and their office numbers. I scrolled until I reached Rayna Willows - Office 421. "There," I whispered to myself, and tapped the '4' button.

"What are you going to do?" I asked her, not sure if I wanted to know the answer.

"I'll keep security occupied," she said with a wink. "Now go get your moonstone back!"

The elevator dinged and the door slid open. With Martin at my side, I took a deep breath and stepped out into the lobby. Grandma stayed in the elevator, waving as the doors closed and she continued to ascend. I let out a breath and looked around.

Here goes nothing.

Nine

My heart pounded as I looked for office 421. This floor was much quieter than the main level. I didn't see anyone else at all as we walked the sterile corridors. After turning a few corners, I stood in front of the door marked 421. There was even a name plate next to the door that confirmed my suspicion: "Rayna Willows".

"This is it," I breathed.

Martin looked up at me. "You ready?"

I swallowed. "Yeah. Let's do this."

I held my breath and knocked on the door, waiting for someone to answer. I heard a muffled voice inside. "Yes?"

Clearing my throat, I answered. "I have a delivery for Miss Willows?"

The door swung open. Standing there, in a crisp white lab coat and blue pants, was none other than Rayna herself. Her expression when she recognized me could have frozen the ocean.

"What are you doing here?!" She hissed. "How did you even get here in the first place?"

"That's the wrong question." I dug into my pocket and pulled out the amulet I'd found at the library. "I think you'll be wanting this back. But first, I have a few questions of my own."

Rayna's eyes nearly bugged out of her head. "How did--where did you find that? I've been looking all over for it! Did you steal it?"

I yanked it just out of her reach. "You mean like you stole my moonstone?"

She recoiled, her face pale beneath her makeup. "I don't know what you're talking about."

I wasn't going to back down that easily. "Martin, go search the office." Before she could stop him, he bolted past her. "If my moonstone is in there, he'll find it. And if he does, it will look very bad for you, now won't it?"

Her mouth dropped and her lips quivered with rage. "What do you want from me? Why are you doing this to me?"

It was so ridiculous I almost laughed. Now SHE was playing the victim. That's rich!

"I'm not doing anything," I told her. "In fact, I'm the one who wants something from you. Answer some questions and we can both walk away without getting the authorities involved."

She stared at me with her jaw clenched, but she couldn't hide the fear in her eyes. "And what would those questions be?"

"Let me in, and we can talk like adults." I gestured at the door. "Or you can just call security."

I saw a flicker of movement behind her as Martin returned with a small, pearly-blue stone clutched gently in his jaws.

Victory.

"The moonstone is there, Rayna." I pointed. "Now you want to tell me why you have it or should I go ahead and call the police?"

She shook her head. "No...no, please..."

I shrugged. "Fine. I'll wait here while you get your story straight."

Rayna craned her neck around me, eyes flicking back and forth down the hallway. Probably looking to see if anyone else heard us. Finally, she clenched her jaw and opened the door a little further. "Come in."

The office was not at all what I expected. The room was completely bare save for a stack of cardboard boxes against one wall. Only a small, nondescript desk huddled against the far window. Was she...going somewhere?

"Why's everything in boxes?" I asked. "Let me guess, you got a big new promotion and they're giving you a bigger and better office?"

Rayna's carefully put together demeanor slipped, just a little. Worry lines creased her face and she frowned. "Not exactly."

That's when it dawned on me. "Rayna..." I started. I thought I would feel some sort of triumph, but I didn't. It was a cold, sickening emptiness. "Did you lose your job?"

Rayna's voice cracked. "What, you're going to tell me what a disappointment I am too?" She crossed her arms. "I have enough of that from my family, thank you very much."

I froze. My mom always told me there was more to people than met the eye, but never had I seen it so clearly before. I was still mad, sure, but I felt something else I hadn't expected. I actually felt bad for her.

I held out the amulet she'd lost and placed it on the desk. I pushed it toward her, as a gesture of goodwill. "Is that why you always seemed so eager to show off?"

She gulped. Nodded. "My parents were on the Alchemical Research Team, too, you know. Going back generations. They wanted me to do the same. Never really had any other choice." Rayna sighed and her shoulders slumped. "They'd been pushing me for so long. You can't know what that's like." Her expression grew cold and she turned away. "When they found out I lost my job, they..." She fiddled with her hands and then dropped them to her sides. "Well, they weren't happy. I can say that much."

"And you thought having the seat of honor at the Festival might change that?" I could kind of see where she was coming from, but it was a stretch to say the least.

She looked up sharply and glared at me. "You don't know anything about my life!"

"You're right." I held up my hands. "I don't. But it's clear that you're hurting."

Rayna scoffed. "What do you care? I've been nothing but mean to you."

That gave me pause. She was right, so why was I trying to help her? My mother's words rang in my ears at that exact moment. 'Be kind. Everyone you meet is fighting some kind of battle.'

I took a deep breath. "Look," I said. "I'm sorry you've been going through all of this. It didn't give you any right to take my moonstone, though. What did you hope to achieve by making me look bad?" I shook my head. "It doesn't add up."

"I needed a distraction," she said bitterly. "It all sounds so stupid now, but I thought if you 'lost' your moonstone, no one would even find it suspicious. They all know you have a habit of losing things, but if I just so happened to 'find' it at the right time..." Rayna sighed. "It was my own misguided plan to be a hero."

I wasn't quite following. "Hero?"

"If I were the one to 'save the day', so to speak, maybe I could save face with not only my family, but my boss." She shrugged helplessly. "I spent so long trying to make myself look good to everyone else, that I forgot what was important. The truth is, I was just a little bit jealous of you."

"Of me?" I blinked. "Why?"

"You have a job. A family that loves you. Even a familiar. And I...don't. Not anymore." Tears ringed her eyes and she sniffed. "I'm sorry for being so mean to you."

"And?" Martin cut in. He stood between us with his tail pointed straight toward the sky.

"And I'm sorry I stole your moonstone." Rayna's voice was soft and small. "Th-thank you for listening. And thank you for bringing my amulet back."

The two of us stared at each other. I didn't know what to say. For once, we weren't two opposites butting heads and trying to get the best of one another. I was still hurt, but I saw a different side of her that I hadn't before.

"It's an incredible piece of work," I mentioned, nodding at it. "Did you make it yourself?"

Rayna picked it up and gazed at the engravings, her eyes far away. "In a way. It's been passed down in my family for generations. We all added our own special touch to it. So you can imagine how I felt when I realized it was gone."

Another strange feeling -- sympathy -- bloomed through me. I didn't know exactly what she was going through, but there was one thing that I could relate to: that feeling of insecurity. Of not being enough. Of being a disappointment.

"I see."

"So..." Rayna said quietly, staring at her hands. "Are you still going to call the police?"

I thought about it for a moment. "No. I think we can both walk away from this without anyone getting arrested."

She sighed and nodded. "Thank you, then. For listening. And for finding the amulet. I guess things worked out in the end." Rayna flinched. "For you, at least."

"Will you be okay?" I asked, looking around at the boxes again. "I think the Library's hiring again soon, if you're interested."

Rayna shrugged. "I'll manage. I think...I think I need to see where life takes me for a little while. On my terms -- no one else's."

"Okay. Well..." I started. "Good luck out there. And thanks, Rayna."

"For what?" She looked genuinely confused.

"We helped each other, without realizing it. This whole situation made me realize I'd been too hard on myself, as well. We both realized what was important to us." I snorted. "Even if we both made some pretty terrible decisions in the process."

Rayna's expression softened. "I suppose you're right."

"Will I see you at the Festival?" I asked, turning for the door. "I could use some help putting up the decorations."

"You want ME to help?" Her voice rose an octave. "After what I did? Why?"

"Because you're one of the best crafters in town. Your amulet alone is proof of that. And because I believe in second chances. What do you say?" I held my hand out and waited for her to take it.

I expected Rayna to reject me outright, but she actually took my hand. "Oh, what the heck. It'll give me something to do. And hey, maybe I'll be able to smooth things over with my parents, too. Just...don't tell anyone what happened here, all right? I've got a reputation to uphold."

I laughed. That was the Rayna I knew. "You help me, I help you. Deal?"

"Deal."

We shook and I left her office. Martin followed close behind. When we made it back to the elevators, he finally spoke up.

"What were you thinking, letting her get away with it like that? Do you not remember all the times she tried to belittle you?"

"Yeah, I still do. But what would getting her in trouble have achieved?" I thought for a moment. Why HAD I extended such kindness to her? "Well, that, and I do really need help with the Festival. Figured it's a win-win."

Martin snickered. "If you say so."

The elevator doors opened at last. I was about to step in when I realized there was someone already in there.

"Oh, look what timing!" Grandma Sam ushered us inside. Her face was flushed and her clothes a bit rumpled. I didn't want to know what kind of 'distraction' she'd cooked up with the security guy. "Did you get what you needed?"

"Yeah," I said with a smile, holding up my moonstone to show her.

"That's my girl!" She clapped and hugged me. "Now, let's get you back to the library."

My stomach did a few preemptive flip-flops. Oh no. Not the scooter again!

As the doors dinged closed and we descended, I couldn't help but laugh. We were together, we were safe, and most of all, I had my moonstone back. Maybe things weren't so bad after all.

Epilogue – The Festival

Dear Diary,

The Festival was a huge success! Rayna was a great help with the decorations -- did you know that she can make these paper dragon lanterns that actually fly? It was amazing! The Moonstone Ritual went off without a hitch, and as the Moon Goddess bathed us in her light, I never felt so proud. All my family were there, and so many of my friends, too. It was an important night for us all, but it also reminded me of one thing: I'm not alone. And maybe I'm not such a bad witch after all.

Even in the days after the Festival, people kept approaching me at the library to thank me for all my work. I told them the same thing every time -- it was a team effort. The whole town came together for this one. I just happened to be the host this time. My boss was at the Festival too, you know. He was so impressed with my work, he called me into the office the next day. I was so afraid he was going to fire me or something, but he gave me a raise!

And then there's Martin. You see, I was doing some research on the Library's history before the Festival, and I found out that it used to belong to a very famous wizard by the same name. I wonder if they're related?

Anyway, he's doing well. Fat and happy, as per usual. When he's not sleeping, he's helping me at home or with the books. Miss Everness, one of the preservation ladies, accidentally left a door open one night and a bunch of mice came in to get out of the cold. Martin had a field day with that, let me tell you. They even gave him an honorary title: Hunter-in-Chief.

Rayna's doing all right. We haven't talked much since the Festival, but she hasn't come by to harass me a single time since our encounter at the ARL. From what I hear, she got a job at the local Academy and is continuing her research over there. No word on her family situation, but the few times I've seen her, she seems happier. And that's a start.

I've been working hard, trying to keep up with everything. It's a busy life, but it's a full one. Full of laughter and family and magic and love. I don't think I'll ever get tired of it.

I still lose things here and there -- don't worry. That part of me hasn't changed. Martin and I have been working on a new system to help me keep track of things, though. That seems to be helping. What HAS changed is the way I view myself. I'm no longer the frail, clumsy loser of a witch I thought I was. I'm a woman who has a purpose, and a place, and a family that loves her.

That's all that matters, in the end.

From Morgan Vale: I wanted to personally take a moment and thank you for reading this book. I know there are lots of choices out there, so it means a lot that you chose to spend this time with me.

If you enjoyed this book, here's another FREE story by Morgan Vale to get you started:

Ghosts and Garlands

You can find more of Morgan's books on Amazon. Thank you for reading!

www.ingramcontent.com/pod-product-compliance
Lightning Source LLC
Chambersburg PA
CBHW051242160726
47994CB00002B/990